T0244991

VENOM

VENOM

Saneh Sangsuk

Translated from the Thai
by Mui Poopoksakul

DEEP VELLUM PUBLISHING
DALLAS, TEXAS

Deep Vellum Publishing
3000 Commerce Street, Dallas, Texas 75226
deepvellum.org · @deepvellum

Deep Vellum is a 501c3 nonprofit literary arts organization founded in 2013 with the
mission to bring the world into conversation through literature.

Originally published as *Asorraphit* (อสรพิษ)
by Maew Kraow Press (สำนักพิมพ์แมวคราว)
(Prachuap Khiri Khan, Thailand)
Published in the United Kingdom as *Venom* in 2023
by Peirene Press Ltd (Bath, UK)

First US edition, 2024

Support for this publication has been provided in part by grants
from the National Endowment for the Arts, the Texas Commission
on the Arts, the City of Dallas Office of Arts and Culture, the Communities
Foundation of Texas, the Addy Foundation, and English PEN.

LIBRARY OF CONGRESS CATALOGING-IN-PUBLICATION DATA
Names: Saneh Sangsuk, author. | Poopoksakul, Mui, translator.
Title: Venom / Saneh Sangsuk ; translated from the Thai by Mui Poopoksakul.
Other titles: 'Asŏrraphit. English
Description: Dallas, Texas : Deep Vellum Publishing, 2024.
Identifiers: LCCN 2024012055 (print) | LCCN 2024012056 (ebook) | ISBN
9781646053506 (paperback) | ISBN 9781646053629 (ebook)
Subjects: LCGFT: Short stories.
Classification: LCC PL4209.D28 A9813 2024 (print) | LCC PL4209.D28
(ebook) | DDC 895.9/134--dc23/eng/20240508
LC record available at https://lccn.loc.gov/2024012055
LC ebook record available at https://lccn.loc.gov/2024012056

Cover art and design by Emily Mahon
Interior layout and typesetting by Andrea García Flores

Printed in the United States of America

EVENING WAS ALREADY NEAR. The sun wasn't so strong now; the orb itself, flushed a deep red, had taken on a softer and gentler quality. The sky was clear as a crystal dome. Over the horizon to the west, the clouds of summer, met from behind by sunlight, glowed strange and lustrous and beautiful. The assortment of their shapes stirred the boy's imagination: he sat there gazing at those clouds as though deep in a meditative state. In them, he saw a range of overlapping mountains, a dense forest, a big lone tree whose limbs had been snapped off by a storm, a hillock shaped like a woman laid on her side.

He'd never shared the contents of his imagination with anyone, not even his close friends, the other boys out grazing their oxen with him now, who were presently engrossed in playing with the pinwheels they'd fashioned out of the umbrella sedge that grew by the pond. He looked on at his oxen feeding alongside his friends'. As his eyes passed over his animals, he counted them: all eight were there, where they were supposed to be.

He had named all of his oxen himself—it was a special privilege his parents had given him, and he'd spent a great deal of thought and care on naming each ox. The first four had names related to the world he saw around him every day: Field, Bank, Jungle and Mountain —Toong, Tah, Pah and Khao. He liked the ring of that rhyme and how it sounded like it could be poetry. The next two were named after gemstones: Pet and Ploy —Diamond and Sapphire—and this past year, when his father had bought two more male calves, he'd had their names ready to go: Ngeun and Tong—Silver and Gold. Pet, Ploy, Ngeun and Tong. He liked the ring of that alliteration, too, and how it sounded like it could be poetry. Every time his parents found out the name he'd given an ox, they smiled and simply accepted it and proceeded to use the name, like when his father had said one evening, *All right, Toong, Tah, it's time for you two to go to your shed. You should know by now where you sleep at night*, or like when his mother had said one evening, *Ngeun, Tong, it's time for you to grow up—I'm about to teach you to how to plow.* His parents were pleased to have all eight of their oxen be christened with such neat, lovely names, and he was pleased to make his parents happy. He was immensely attached to the eight oxen —had he not been the one to name them, their bond most likely wouldn't have been the same. He was their friend and at the same time their master, and they accepted him as such. He loved all his oxen. He took great care not to favor or disfavor any of them. During the planting season, his father plowed and harrowed using Toong and Tah, while his mother plowed and harrowed using Pah and Khao, keeping Pet and Ploy as spares to be substituted when one of the other pairs became worn out or injured from the back-breaking work. But he did his best to love the oxen equally— Ngeun and Tong, the youngest, weren't the only ones to receive his attention. Every day, after their work in the fields was finished, he bathed each of them meticulously and brought each of them a sheaf of fresh-cut grass.

He wanted his parents to buy another ox—or, better yet, two more. In his spare time, he liked to think up names for his future oxen.

He'd turned ten this past February, and had recently finished his final year of school, fourth grade. His friends in the village, both boys and girls, called him Gimp. At school, back when he had still been enrolled, his classmates also called him Gimp. Some of the adults in the village called him Gimp as well. This was because his right arm, from the shoulder down, was atrophied and hung stiffly by his side. The elbow couldn't be bent, and all five of the fingers were completely rigid and useless—their only position was straight out; he couldn't spread them or make a fist. His right shoulder, too, sloped down and looked scrawny and frail. His left arm, though, was sturdy and powerful, the fingers on that hand long and solid and agile. His left shoulder was also strong and nicely filled out. In a fight, he was always ready to take on another child his size—or even one a little bigger—and though he had only one good arm, he always fought as if to the death.

Song Waad took great delight in calling him Gimp,

fucking Gimp, son of a bitch Gimp, saying his name with disdain and hatred, relishing the opportunity to remind himself and other people in the village of the boy's imperfection. Song Waad was a medium, a man of about fifty, short and stocky, with a dark, dark complexion. Before, he used to be known simply as Waad, or, even more coarsely, Ai Waad, but then one day five years ago, he told everyone in the village that the Patron Goddess of Praeknamdang had expressed the wish to have him serve as her medium, and he alone could invite her spirit into his body, and he could do this any time he liked. A lot of people, both in their village of Praeknamdang and in nearby communities, believed him. Thus, plain old Waad became Song Waad, earning himself the title of medium, and little by little he grew more prosperous, no longer having to lift a finger to farm or raise cattle or pigs. During his sessions channeling the Goddess, he would wear white bloomers and a white blouse with long sleeves, and over the blouse a white sabai top with the loose end thrown over his shoulder, and he would tuck a red flower behind his ear. He would speak with his voice pitched high and sweet like a woman's and fill his speech with rare, archaic words few could understand, and his mannerisms would morph into a woman's. What's more, he could perform the most unusual dances and perform them with such feminine grace. His whole act had a mystical aura to it and was convincing. Song Waad, therefore, had become a person of power and influence in the village, and he was always ready to wield the power and influence he possessed.

Among the fields of Praeknamdang sat several empty tracts of land; they'd been designated as public property, to be used for the good of all, but Song Waad had high-handedly gone and occupied those plots, put up fences and planted trees, with the view to one day gaining ownership rights over the land. The boy's father had called Song Waad's actions selfish, and he'd protested. But Song Waad had stood his ground and continued to make use of those parcels of land, so that eventually, when the government was ready to issue deeds, he'd be in the position to claim to officials that, as the person who had long made use of the plots, he deserved to be considered their sole rightful owner.

His status as the medium of the Patron Goddess of

Praeknamdang made people fear and revere him. But the father of the boy with the bad arm didn't believe Waad was truly the medium of the Patron Goddess. What his father often said was, *Ai Waad can't fool anybody but the stupid.* His mother, too, never showed Song Waad enough deference for his liking. That was the reason Song Waad didn't like his parents and, by extension, didn't like him. And that dislike had turned into full-blown hatred the day he had hit Song Waad's son, giving the kid a big, swollen black eye (he'd thrown his hardest punch, never mind that the other boy outweighed him by quite a bit. What was he supposed to do? That bully had picked a fight with him first). Song Waad always said that disrespecting the medium of the Goddess of Praeknamdang was tantamount to disrespecting the Goddess herself: whoever dared to commit such blasphemy was bound to meet with tragedy sooner or later. So when, two years ago, he'd fallen off a toddy palm, broken his right arm and lost the use of it, Song Waad was clear: that had been the invisible hand of the Goddess of Praeknamdang, shoving him.

Two years earlier—he had been eight—one day

early in the monsoon season, he was out grazing his oxen in the fields when he spotted a toddy palm bearing young fruit, which he thought just right for his mother's curry. The tree was barely mature, standing only six meters tall or so. This palm, unlike most, didn't have a bamboo pole tied to it, which would have made it easier to get up. He decided to climb it nevertheless.

He unsheathed the knife he wore at his waist and put the blade between his teeth and, to rid his soles of the season's mud, wiped them on the damp grass. Then up he expertly climbed, until he was a short reach away from the palm's crown. He wasn't at all nervous and didn't for a second consider it risky—he'd climbed palms taller than this before. The crown of the tree was packed with brown leaf sheaths which had yet to drop and blocked his passage further up. Without tearing them off, he wouldn't be able to access the fruit and slice down a cluster. So, he wrapped his left arm around the palm's trunk, pressed the soles of his feet against it to support his weight, and with his free hand went to snatch a dry sheath dangling above his head. The palm was slick all over with a slime of green mold. The sheath, which he'd thought would need a yank, in fact detached itself more readily than he'd anticipated. He'd been about to say to himself, *Well, this stuff wasn't so hard to get rid of*, but by mid-sentence he was already plummeting downward, together with that leaf sheath. Frightened, he screamed, his carry knife slipping out of his mouth. He hit the ground hard, landing on his right side, and he heard a crack—unmistakably his right arm breaking. He felt the wind knocked out of his gut, then an onslaught of intense pain. Clench-jawed, he tossed and turned on the ground, and in that manner he lay past when the sun had dropped below the edges of the fields.

His oxen (there were only six of them at the time) refused to leave him behind and return to their shed, although dusk was already upon them. They all came and gathered around him; they bellowed repeatedly and, upset, huffed as they nudged him with their noses and licked his face and person with their rough, slobbery tongues.

The evening star was already visible in the sky by the time his father found him at the scene, flat on the ground, drawing shallow breaths, body covered in mud, right arm broken at the elbow and hanging limply, right shoulder out of joint, yet still clench-jawed and not a tear in his eyes. The hospital was too far away, as was Laad Po Temple, where Luang Paw Ring, the reputed bone doctor, could be found. For months, he had had to drink pennywort juice to relieve the tenderness; still, his right arm and the shoulder on that side never regained their function. That was how he came to be called Gimp. That was also what gave Song Waad the excuse to oft repeat that the accident was the Goddess of Praeknamdang striking back at him and his family for their failure to accord her medium due respect. Quite a few people believed Song Waad's assertion, and the villagers grew to fear and revere the medium even more.

But his mother and father never called him Gimp. Neither did Grannie Pluppleung, the midwife, or Luang Paw Tien, the abbot of Praeknamdang Temple, and he'd always felt gratitude towards these people. His parents had given him life and had raised him, Grannie Pluppleung had delivered him and cut his umbilical cord, and Luang Paw Tien had been kind enough to give him a name.

Not long after the accident, his father had said to him, *Do you want to learn how to ride a bike? I'll teach you.* He'd nodded and then practiced on his father's huge bicycle, which was much too tall, almost taller than him. On top of that, the bicycle had a crossbar; he'd had to hunch under the metal tube, set his feet on the pedals and hang onto the handlebars with his left hand and his bad right arm—it was a terribly awkward way to learn to ride a bike. In their front yard, where you could kick up a lot of dust, he'd fallen again and again and struggled back up again and again, hurt himself over and over, coming away with cuts and scratches on his legs, his arms, and even his face. In the end, he could ride the bike anywhere he pleased, although it was more for his father than for himself that he'd learned to ride.

As though he were already a grown-up, at the arrival of the rainy season his father would say to him, *Which paddy field do you think we should plow first?* His mother, too, consulted him on all kinds of matters. She would say to him, *My Pah and Khao have really taken a beating. What do you say, should I take Ngeun and Tong out tomorrow instead?* By guiding his left hand, his mother taught him to write all over again, putting up with his moods as he trained himself to form letters and vowels anew: □, □, □, □. His mother would say to him, *You can do this. Before long, you're going to be able to write better and with nicer handwriting than all the other kids.*

Grannie Pluppleung would say to him, *Come here, child, can you show me your little snakehead?* Then she would wrestle him and pin him down and pull his shorts off his bottom to inspect his little snakehead and say: *Some parts of your body may be no good, but your little snakehead is just fine, and I hope, in time, it will grow into an impressive snakehead.* Which embarrassed him. He got embarrassed every time Grannie Pluppleung did and said those things to him. But he understood she meant well and only wished to give him encouragement.

Luang Paw Tien paid him special attention too, and would take him aside and say to him, *Is it true you're already helping your parents out in the fields?*; or, *Wah, is it true you can already ride a bike?*; or, *Is it true you can already write left-handed? Show me, transcribe the Chinabanchon spell from this book here into this notebook for me.*

His parents and Grannie Pluppleung and Luang Paw Tien—who never, ever called him Gimp—were always gentle towards him, and they were always patient with him when he did something wrong. For this reason, they were the people he loved the most. He had tried to make himself love others as well, but he realized that he still loved the people who were good to him more than he loved the rest of them. He also realized that he despised Song Waad, and that Song Waad likewise despised him. That bothered him a great deal.

On the festival night of Loy Krathong, he'd gone out to the stream behind his house, to the spot where the dock was, under the large tamarind tree. There, he'd raised his krathong float to his head, paid honor to Mae Phra Kongka of the waters, asked for her forgiveness, and prayed she grant him a few wishes as well. He prayed to Mae Phra Kongka for his parents to receive a bountiful harvest and for their rice to fetch a good price; for Grannie Pluppleung, who was about to move away from Praeknamdang to go and live with her grandson in the district of Tha Gwian Gampaeng Hak, not to move just yet; for Luang Paw Tien, who by that time was ailing on and off due to his advanced age, to enjoy good health and many more years of life; and lastly he prayed that he might be rid of his hatred of Song Waad and that Song Waad might be rid of his hatred of him. Then he lit the candle and joss sticks on his float and set the float on the water, watching as the swollen stream carried it away.

A couple of days after Loy Krathong, when Luang Paw Tien stopped by his house on his alms round, he asked Luang Paw Tien: *Luang Paw, on Loy Krathong night, I prayed to Mae Kongka, asking her for a few things . . . these prayers people make, do they ever come true?* Luang Paw Tien didn't give him an answer right away, but looked at him and asked: *Well, what were the things you prayed for?* Once he had told Luang Paw Tien, the monk smiled and said, *Your prayers will be answered, all of them will be answered.*

NOW THE SUN WAS EVEN WEAKER. Above the westerly horizon, the sky glowed a purplish red. The clouds continued to shift shape; bursts of wind blew on through the pastures. The boy looked at the vast, forlorn fields: a sprawl of golden brown extending as far as the eye could see, mottled with dabs of somber green where there were patches of scrub or toddy palm groves. He looked at the ox-cart path, at the temple, and at the village beyond them. It was all familiar landscape to him. He looked at his oxen and counted: all were there. His friends, having grown bored of playing with their pinwheels, were now stood in a circle kicking around a takraw ball, a frayed old thing made of rattan, and even though they didn't particularly care about the game they still managed to make a lot of noise. Another day at the tail end of a lazy summer was about to pass. He stretched, then stood up, and as he did tore off four or five fistfuls of rice stubble to take with him. Then he wandered towards the pond that lay nearby.

The pond, sitting in the middle of the sweeping fields, was great in width and length as well as in depth and age. It had been there since time immemorial, dug many years ago to store irrigation water for the paddies. The pond had been public property, but recently Song Waad had appropriated it for himself. Along all four sides, the pond was framed by a dense growth of trees of different sizes, with festoons of vines dangling from them. It had become much shallower given the season, its surface strewn with water lettuce, duckweed, water primrose and morning glory. Within the bamboo grove on its northern side was a shrine dedicated to the Patron Goddess of Praeknamdang, made of wood and in the form of a miniature Thai house. Inside the shrine, there was a carved wooden figurine depicting a woman sitting primly on the ground with her legs folded to the side. She wore a sarong that grazed the top of her feet and a sabai top covering one of her shoulders. The statuette had a comely face, but her expression was stern and forbidding. Before her stood an incense burner, a candle rack and a vase holding dry flowers. As a matter of fact, there was already a shrine to the Patron Goddess, in the north of the village, but Song Waad had claimed that the Goddess wished for a new one to be constructed. He then arranged to have the new shrine built next to this pond and seized the opportunity at the same time to plant banana and coconut trees along one stretch, on the pond's eastern side, to mark his territory.

The boy with the bad arm headed towards the big trees that lined the pond on the shrine side. Like an invitation, the fresh, moist air from the water and surrounding trees wafted over to him. He felt as though he were being drawn into a sanctuary of calm the nearer he went. The only sounds came from the wind brushing through the trees, from the bamboo creaking as its culms rubbed together, or from the hiss of rustling leaves. On the ground, dry leaves from that same bamboo lay scattered; beside them, there was nothing but the remains of a tamarind tree, about two arm spans in girth, lying fallen and bare and rotting among the brown foliage. The boy sat down on the base of that dead tree and regarded the shrine for a while. He and his friends used to always come to hang out and play by this pond. They used to fish and catch shrimp here and used to collect wild mangoes to snack on. But after the shrine was erected, the pond (or so Song Waad claimed) became property of the Goddess, and therefore whatever life its water nurtured, and whatever the trees along its fringes bore, also belonged to her. And the shrine itself seemed an uncanny thing; it possessed and radiated an aura that was somehow sinister and foreboding. He and his friends, like the rest of the village, didn't visit the area much anymore.

Clutching a bundle of rice stubble in his left fist, the boy began forming figures in the shape of people. His right arm was used to prop them up, while his feet and mouth were called upon to help out from time to time. In all, there were six human figures. All were much wanting in neatness of workmanship, but each represented a great deal of care and effort. This one here was an eremite; this one a king; these two princes; and then there were the two buffoons, Gaew and Gae. The eremite, the king and the two princes were far off the mark in terms of verisimilitude, but with Gaew and Gae he knew he'd done himself proud—the two buffoons were commoners, they didn't have to look like characters from a fairy tale. Gaew had a face and hairdo that made him resemble a cow. Gae's face was reminiscent of a crocodile.

He was thinking he'd stage a shadow puppet show. He took playing very seriously—no matter the game, he always put his heart and soul into it. He loved watching shadow plays. Whenever a troupe came to town, either to Praeknamdang or a nearby village, he never missed a show. He liked to climb up backstage and watch the puppeteer and musicians at work. Observing the puppeteer, he was always in awe: the master seated meditation-style beneath a flood of light, his body drenched in sweat, his deft hands seesawing as he maneuvered the puppets, his lips all the while singing or reciting poetry or speaking lines of dialogue. The boy knew scores of different songs and poems and gags from various shadow plays by heart. His dream was to become a shadow puppeteer when he grew up, lame arm be damned.

So it was that he situated himself with his back to the sinking sun, which was about to meet the horizon. The sun would serve as his barn lantern; the blankness before him would serve as his screen. He stuck the shaft of his eremite puppet into a split in a branch of the dead tamarind, and he was ready now to commence the wai khru ceremony; you had first to pay homage to the teachers of the art. Though he had no audience, he was undeterred—he knew that his friends, still half-heartedly passing that takraw ball back and forth, would eventually wind up coming over to watch his performance. That was the way it always went. Every time he staged a shadow play, everyone eyed him with a mix of jealousy and admiration. In this regard, none of his friends could hold a candle to him, because one day he was going to become the Great Gimpy-Armed Shadow Puppeteer, whose wizardry would keep an audience a thousand strong glued to their seats from dusk till dawn.

Without further ado, he went ahead and began reciting the ode to the teachers, his voice resonant and clear as a bell:

With hands placed on top of my pate,
I dedicate my play unto you,
My starving minstrel teacher who
Said adieu to food for his art.
Bless my song, oh undertaker,
My teacher well-versed in the dark.
Be my guide, pirate, you ship shark
Who embarks just to show machismo.
I salute and worship all of you,
My teachers who gamble day and night.
Coin toss, dice roll, that's your might.
It's your fight to play red or black.

(He paused, clearing his throat, then went on with that roast of a paean.)

Let my song be in your honor:
Card players in games of all sorts,
Hash masters who smoke for a sport,
Crooks who extort and snatch purse and pouch.
Instruct me, snake oil peddler,
Shameless liar with truth so carefree

Turn will he blank air into monkey.
But it's he I play tribute to.

His friends had wandered over now. There were seven of them altogether, each fried dark by the sun, dressed in faded, patched-up, shabby-looking clothes, their feet all shoeless, each wearing a woven floppy hat and carrying a staff. Some stood in front of him, while others sat on the ground. All of them were rapt, listening intently. Some were trying to remember his every word and his every gesture. In the past, some had even begged him to write the verses down on a piece of paper, so they could go off and memorize the lines and sing them on their own. But he'd refused—that was something that had taken him a lot of time and a lot of effort to learn. Some had pestered him to repeat the words to them, but there was no way he was going to give in. He could see in his friends' eyes their hunger for entertainment; children are always seduced by silly rhymes. And so he kept going with the next few verses:

Guide me high on opium, my teacher

Who's sober on less than three hits;
Neither ganja nor kratom will he quit—
May my writ please you to no end.

That, so far, was no more than the wai khru ode, and already it was obvious the play was going to be a cheeky one. Then, without further ado, he got on with the tale itself, telling of a king—the father of the two princes who would turn out to be the heroes. He projected his voice as he sang, keeping time with the pipers and drummers inside his head. His voice was so loud that his oxen turned to look.

Once, perhaps twice, upon a time,
Was a prime dominion of one king
Whose subjects so poor the only thing
Flavoring their rice was plain salt.
Fish bones were their one luxury.
More richly couldn't be named their king:
Prosperus, with its glorious ring,
He reigning over his grand land.

The story hadn't yet come to the two princes, the main characters, but his two prince puppets were ready and raring to prance around onstage. The story hadn't yet come to Gaew and Gae either, but his two buffoon puppets were also ready and raring to prance around onstage. Gaew and Gae were both itching to drop their best jokes for the audience, but the sun would probably dip below the horizon before they had much chance to liven things up. At that point, it would be time for him to herd his oxen back home, and he'd refuse to carry on with the show even if his friends implored him to—*No way*. He might not even resume the show tomorrow evening. He'd only do it when it suited his mood. In that moment, the boy could envision his future self: a grown man with swarthy skin, with defined facial features, backstage at a shadow puppet theater, dripping sweat under the barn lantern's light, working the puppets and making those perforated cowhide cut-outs come to life with his magic; below him at least a thousand theatergoers who stood ready to laugh or cry with the puppets as he spun out the yarns of their fates; the name carried on the frame over the screen belonging to him, the illustrious shadow puppeteer. But that was all in the future. He cleared his throat again—just a little—and continued with the next stanzas, which detailed the grandeur of the king's capital:

His vast realm sprawled wide, for forearms.
Wielding charm were its moat, towers, walls,
But up them prickled vines did high crawl,
The gates all blackened with torch soot.
The keep leaned and rocked rickety;
A princely hand's wave could make it fall.
Wooden boards patched holes in its walls,
But it all was jolly to the king.

That moment, a giant snake, a female king cobra, angrily reared up its head from a burrow concealed beneath the big rotting tamarind tree the boy had been sitting on. The creature had the girth of a grown man's thigh; its dorsal side was jet black, its underside a yellowish grey.

It was nearly dusk. The snake had been waiting a long time to come out of its nest to go and hunt for food, but the noises above its burrow—feet stomping

on the ground, bodies moving, laughter, a voice chant-
ing in rhymes—wouldn't quiet down. It had already
sneaked up several times, flicking its tongue in and out
while spying on the scene. These small humans, every
one an enemy full of both danger and cowardice, each
had a bamboo stick well gripped in their hand. Luckily,
these rascals hadn't brought along dogs—dogs were an
adversary snakes always preferred to avoid. But even
when forced to flee, a snake fled with dignity; it did so
unhurriedly, foregoing haste in favor of defiance while
exuding malice through every part of its body, through
every twist of its movement. It had faith in its fangs
and its venom. This was the snake's domain. The nest
and the ground above its mouth were territory it was
protective of. Here, atop this rotting tamarind log, was
where it would come and perch at night time to bathe
in the dew and be stroked by the breeze. The trespass
onto its turf by these small humans enraged it. The five
eggs stacked neatly in tiers within its nest made it fear-
less, made it willing to put its life on the line, even. That
it had appeared in that manner meant the snake had
already declared war, and that war, commanded by its

deepest instincts, was going to be a decisive one. It was
ready to strike.

Within the blink of an eye, the snake had reared up
high enough to reveal a length of nearly four meters.
It rocked from side to side and spread its hood wide,
the force seething within every particle of its being. It
threatened with hisses that sounded like an anthem
of death. It could hear the small humans hotfooting it
away, screaming in chaos. It could hear the oxen stam-
peding away as well, surely with their ears pricked, tails
lifted, eyes popping out of their heads.

Of the little humans, only one now remained. It was
this one that had been sitting on the log right above its
nest, *this* one that had been the source of the ceaseless
yelling earlier, *this* one that the snake had marked as its
target from the start. It was a small human with imper-
fections, its right arm unnaturally shrunken, the fingers
of its right hand locked in full extension, its puny right
shoulder sloping down, with six straw figures lying scattered by its feet. As the snake stretched up higher, the
little human sprang up as well. The little human's eyes
were wide, its mouth agape and stuffed with the roar

of silence. It was too startled to even run for its life; its head had been deep in its own fun and games. The other little humans were yelling to try to help it regain its wits: *Run, Gimp, run!* But their voices echoed over to him like something in a dream, and the body of the little human showed not a movement before the big snake. The snake's fury surged. It reared up even higher, pitched its head back, arched its body until it was like a bow stretched to the limit, and its mouth yawned wide, displaying the gleaming curves of its fangs. The wind, relentless, howled through the fields. The bottom arc of the sun had joined the horizon now. From afar, there came the doleful sound of calves crying for their mother, while above, a Brahminy kite gliding high up in the sky squawked in hunger as it made its way back to its well-hidden nest. Before the kite was even out of earshot, the snake moved to strike.

The only thing the boy saw—a mere arm's length away from him—was an object darting at his face; the only thought he registered was that the snake was about to bite him. He squeezed his eyes shut and leaned back, bracing himself. Next, he thought: *pain, death, pain, death, fear, the end*—words that flashed through his head. And he saw himself, under the starlight, staggering in pain along the cracked surface of the vast fields, then collapsing, then writhing in misery under the influence of the snake's venom, and then dying an excruciating death to become a ghost guarding those very fields. The winds of those pastures would blow through him without him being able to feel them any longer, and next he thought: *Mom, Dad, Grannie Pluppleung, Luang Paw Tien, our paddy fields, our oxen,* and he saw everything his mind conjured. Even on that threshold between life and death, he could still call up the names of all his oxen, and he was overcome with sorrow and longing. However, he had unconsciously thrust out his good left arm with the fingers spread wide, and with it had met the neck of the snake charging down at him. The crook of his hand felt like it had been ripped in two. His arm shook and felt completely numb all the way to the shoulder. He'd managed to intercept the attack—with the snake's fangs a mere fraction of a knuckle away from his throat.

The impact of the collision sent him reeling. As he stumbled, he tripped on one of the tamarind's dry limbs, which snapped clean off, and he fell, smashing his face hard into a burl of the fallen tree.

Having failed to strike its target, and with its neck now locked in a chokehold, the snake swiftly threw its coils around the boy. Not a blink had gone by before it had wrapped itself around his left arm, around his trunk, around his right arm, trapping it against his body, and around his two legs, binding them together. But his left arm remained extended, and he clutched the snake's neck tight and kept squeezing, forcing its head away from him. His resistance nearly drove the snake mad with fury. It tightened its grip, its mouth was wide, its fangs bared. It wriggled its neck in an attempt to free itself, but the boy clenched his fingers harder still. Even in that state, the snake still tried to bite him. It went for his hand, and nearly succeeded in burying its fangs in his arm. When he gripped tighter and dug his fingers into its neck even more, the snake responded in kind, squeezing him even harder. Boy and snake struggled, rolling on the ground. Dry bamboo leaves were sent flying up; little bushes and shrubs were crushed, crackling as their branches broke. All the boy with the bad arm knew was that, no matter what, his left hand must never let go of the snake's neck. All the snake knew was that it must do everything in its power to bite its enemy, if only just once, and failing that, it would pour all its strength into constricting its foe, until it suffocated to death.

During their scuffle on the ground, the snake's head was a mere two or three inches away from the boy's face—near enough to smell his breath, tight enough to him to hear his heartbeat, and he too was able to observe the snake up close. There was a strong gamey odor to it, which made his flesh crawl and frightened him even more. The pressure it exerted was beginning to suffocate him, and he felt a dull ache spreading through his entire body. The unsettling coldness of its flesh, along with the repulsive feel of its slithery scales, sent his heart palpitating. He didn't even think about screaming for help; he knew full well there was nobody around to save him. Struggling on the ground, he tried to flip himself upright, because, flat like that, he was at a disadvantage. Though the snake was only squeezing him harder, he got himself onto his knees eventually, and by pressing the snake's neck against the rotting tamarind log he managed to stand up. His every pore was gushing sweat. He didn't know it yet, but when he'd slammed into the burl of that fallen tamarind he'd cut himself above his right eyebrow and inside his mouth. His nostrils did, however, pick up the scent of blood. He spat. He couldn't see the color of the saliva, but its smell and taste—gamey and vaguely salty—let him know there was blood. He blinked. The sweat in his eyes stung, and his vision was blurred.

THE SKY APPEARED DESOLATE. The horizon to the west was still flushed red, though the sun itself was no longer visible. His eight oxen still hadn't gone home to their shed; they'd lingered nearby, uncertain, showing up as dark silhouettes in the fields. The other cowherd boys had tried to help usher them back to the village, but they'd resisted. Maybe it'd been Toong, their leader, who'd been stubborn, which might have prompted the others to be stubborn as well. They were worried about the boy; they could sense that something had happened. Normally, this late in the evening, it would be time for him to lead them back to their shed, and they were waiting for him. They each mooed and mooed and mooed. Out of habit, he counted them: they were all there. That comforted him. With the giant snake still looped tight around him, he tried to walk towards the herd. He could just about manage to stagger. The sky was ever losing its light, and the wind had picked up even further. The evening star was out now, a glimmering white light in the western sky. His eight oxen were huddled close together, and they were still crying *moo, moo, moo,* calling out to him, the master of their lives. He walked towards them . . . and approached closer . . . and closer still. The ears on all eight of them pricked up, their eyes popped wide, and their tails shot out. He wasn't expecting his oxen to be able to help him. He simply thought, *It's twilight now, it's time for them to return to their shed.* Despite the giant snake coiled around him he thought, still, that he must herd them back. Taking them home was his duty. He approached even closer. The eight oxen huffed loudly through their noses and swung their heads wildly, and even after they got a good look at him, they didn't recognize him. That form and that scent weren't what they were used to, weren't what the eight of them were expecting. And so they bolted, scared for their lives, making their way in the direction of the village.

The boy stayed put, watching his oxen sprint off into nightfall's gathering dark. He stood there, hesitating. He ought to go and find his parents. He knew they wouldn't be home but at the temple, helping to saw wood for Luang Paw Tien, as Lung Paw Tien was repairing an old monk's residence near the cemetery. His parents had been helping Luang Paw Tien with the timber for the kuti for days now and had been returning home late, sometimes deciding to stay the night and sleep in the sermon hall. His parents might be able to help him. Luang Paw Tien, too, might be able to help him. He hadn't yet given any thought to how. He was worried about his house; he was worried about his oxen. But first he ought to find either his parents or Luang Paw Tien. In any case, from where he was, the temple was nearer than his home. And so he set out along the ox-cart path, every one of his steps a slow struggle, making his way in the direction of Praeknamdang Temple.

Within the temple grounds, the seven or eight resident dogs flocked together outside the ordination hall growled at him, and the whole gang of them came running towards him, closed in on him from the front, from

SANEH SANGSUK

behind, barking harshly and baring their fangs at him.
He paid them no mind, neither hastening nor slowing
his footsteps. His eyes, with their distant look, were
trained forward.

The dogs dropped the barking as soon as they took
in the amalgam of boy and giant snake. They whimpered
instead now, in fear, their ears pinned to their heads,
their tails, too, tucked between their legs. Each of them
hung back, looking at the others for cues. When he was
four or five steps past them, one of the dogs dragged out
a long howl, and the rest of the pack started howling too,
like they'd seen a ghost. The pigeons cooing under the
eaves of the ordination hall and in the recesses below
the sermon hall's roof broke into loud grunts, then
launched into nervous flights, sending out warnings to
their own kind to beware of the freakish thing below.

The boy cast his eyes over the dark row of kuti
houses, then over the bushes and shrubs little and large,
then over the chain of medlar trees flanking the temple's pond, then over the stupas—there was no one anywhere. He could hear the hum of prayers coming from
afar. He decided to walk up the steps to the main part

of the temple. It was pitch-dark nearly everywhere; the only light he could see came from the prayer hall. There was a soft glow of candles. He could smell joss sticks burning. There, Luang Paw Tien, four senior bhikkhus and two little novices were saying their evening prayers in voices low-pitched and quiet. He stopped to watch them, feeling as though he were dreaming. Luang Paw Tien might have a way of helping him—he'd seen so much of life, was possessed of such vast knowledge and wisdom, and he was a veteran tudong monk, having wandered through countless jungles in his younger years. But with him in the middle of prayers like that, interrupting him would be disrespectful, it would be a sin. If Luang Paw Tien, the other bhikkhus and the novices were to see him in that state, how would those holy men and boys react? It was possible they would scream; perhaps they would bristle in fear, perhaps they'd be so scared they would flee the scene in complete chaos. If that were to happen, the worship would be ruined, and he, the cause of the disruption, would have to bear a grave sin. Therefore, he decided not to disturb Luang Paw Tien and decided not to wait.

He walked back down from the temple, passed the bell tower, turned left before the bridge over the stream in front, and walked along the watercourse, which had dried up for the season. Its bank on this side was crowded with trees. He walked on, heading towards his parents, who were cutting timber in the open area near the graveyard. He could already hear sawing in the distance. And now he could see his parents in the distance as well, aided by the light from their kerosene lamp, which hung from a branch of a great big weeping fig: his mother and father, a country couple toiling away at the task in front of them. His father was in a loose pair of black pants, secured at the waist with a knot, and he was shirtless, his solid, brown torso drenched in sweat. His mother—who rivalled men in their prime with her strength—was in a black sarong and a black long-sleeved shirt, her clothes also soaked in sweat. The two of them stood on either side of the big log they were sawing and worked in a coordinated fashion: when his father pushed the saw, his mother pulled; once it was her turn to push, he did the pulling.

The pack of dogs outside the ordination hall could

still be heard barking and howling, a noise that was both plaintive and eerie. His parents' kerosene lamp cast a light on the fig tree that made its cascade of roots appear like mysterious shadows, and it cast a light on the nearby morgues and graves as well. The morgue houses were brick and mortar structures, standing in a tidy row. Some were sealed shut at the front, meaning they stored coffins inside. Some were empty, dark shadows the only thing to be seen within. Behind and a little beyond the row of morgues were old graves, whose bodies had yet to be exhumed for cremation. Nearly all of those were corpses of poor people, because the remains of the rich were housed inside the morgues. Above each grave there was a marker—a post jammed into the ground with a sign giving the name of the dead. Not a single one of the grave markers stood upright.

In that area, by the graveyard, though you could hear the scratch of saw blade grinding into wood, hear the dogs barking and howling outside the ordination hall, hear grunts coming from the pigeons beneath the sermon hall's eaves and hear the faint hum of the monks' prayers, it was the silence beyond these sounds—an uncommonly thick, weighty silence—that reigned. The hapless boy went to approach his parents. He tried to yell, *Mom! Dad!* but his tongue wouldn't cooperate. His parents' focus remained on the wood they were sawing. He went closer. With sweat pouring, blood dribbling out of the wound on his head, eyes so wide they were protruding, hair standing straight up from his scalp and a giant snake ringed tight around him while his left hand gripped and dug into its neck, he stepped into the light of his parents' kerosene lamp and showed himself to them.

His mother was the first to notice him. She didn't utter a word. She didn't scream. She merely flinched, dropped what she was doing at once, and pointed. Seeing her, his father dropped what he was doing as well and followed her finger with his gaze. He then froze, hands suspended in the air in a manner the boy had never seen before. And when his mother started running like mad back in the direction of the temple, his father started running right behind her. They left their big saw wedged in the log, its two handle ends shivering as though the saw too had been given a fright.

He cut through the cemetery, then started crossing the fields, heading for the ox-cart path and ultimately heading for the village. With surprise, he realized he hadn't been scared at all when he'd walked past those morgues and graves. Normally, he never dared to set foot *near* the graveyard, not even in broad daylight. This time, there had been the dogs' frenzied howling, and the groans of the pigeons on top of it, and yet, slowly and laboriously, he'd made it through, completely impervious. Given the circumstances, he was far less worried about the souls and spirits than becoming one of them.

His parents had probably gone to look for Luang Paw Tien. They'd probably burst into the prayer hall looking like they had seen a ghost. Probably by now they were sitting on the floor panting, their faces and their bodies covered in sweat, their limbs coated in saw-dust, stammering out an account of what they'd just witnessed and thereby wrecking the solemn mood inside the prayer hall. That behavior would be disrespectful; they'd be committing a sin. The prayers might be cut short, and tonight his parents might rather spend the night at the temple, like they'd done before. His parents hadn't shown the slightest sign of recognizing him. If the thought of him had crossed their minds, they'd probably assumed he was home by now, going through his usual routine of putting the oxen in their shed, fetching them water, bringing them straw, and after that boiling up some rice and preparing himself some simple viand. After dinner, he might lounge around and listen to the radio, or he might go dallying in the village, maybe play four or five rounds of checkers with his friends, then go home, shower and go to bed. Even he, in his present situation, could imagine himself in that established routine.

He walked on and came to the ox-cart path. Between the temple and the village—a distance of about three kilometers—there was nothing but paddy fields, scrub-covered land and overgrown rises. The night was moonless. The path looked like a white blur under the starlight.

The wound in his mouth kept bleeding, which meant he had to spit every so often, and the cut over his right eyebrow continued to bleed too. His injuries were more serious than he'd thought. Some first aid might stop the bleeding, but as things were, blood mixed with sweat was running into his eyes and running down his face. The snake seemed to be getting heavier; it seemed to be getting more slippery as well. Above all else, and more pronounced, however, was the animal smell of its flesh, which seemed to have intensified to the point that it was making him queasy. How old might it be? Fifty? Eighty? A hundred? Did it live with a mate? How old might the mate be? Fifty? Eighty? A hundred? And how large was the mate—bigger, smaller or of comparable size? What might it have eaten in its life? Birds? Frogs? Mice? Fish? Wild rabbits? Other snakes? Had it killed a human before? How many? Was it going to eat him too after it managed to bite him, or would it just slither away? The fear wasn't unfounded—he looked at its mouth, at its jaws: if it stretched them wide, it could slowly swallow him, starting with his head, and little by little cram the rest of him down its throat!

One winter evening, when he was six years old, he'd seen something next to his chicken coop that he hadn't been able to take his eyes off, something he'd watched with amazement and trepidation while being sure to stay perfectly hushed: it was a tiny king cobra, not much bigger than his index finger, with its jaws stretched as wide as they would go, attempting the seemingly impossible feat of engulfing a chicken egg. It wasn't inconceivable, then, that this giant king cobra, after biting him, would devour him whole. What did it feel like to be swallowed alive? How potent *was* its venom? What did it truly feel like to be bitten by a snake? The pain must be horrific, the burn must be awful around the wound, and its poison would probably make the victim exceedingly drowsy. How many minutes before a person died after getting bitten by a king cobra? Was it true what they said about king cobras: that the older the snake, the weaker its venom? But even if its poison was less potent, there was no way the boy was going to let it bite him.

The darker the night, the farther he was from other people, and the longer he bled, the more the snake seemed to come alive and the more vicious it seemed. For it, victory was a mere arm's reach away. The boy's unsteady heartbeat, the labored sound of his unsteady breath and the smell of the blood from his wounds, which to it must have been sweet and tantalizing, made it all the more alert, all the more menacing, all the more impatient for a swift victory. As he crossed a shallow creek—the bed of which was sand and whose water came up only to his ankles—it tensed up, once again squeezing him hard, causing him to teeter and nearly lose his footing. He thought his bones must be getting crushed under that brutal pressure. He fought it, he resisted it, he tried to spread his legs further apart, to stay on his feet and keep still, to take a hard, deep breath. He mustn't let himself fall. He knew that if he did, he'd never be able to stand back up. Before he even managed another step, the snake wriggled its upper body again to try to get itself free, to try to get itself in a better position to strike. But in return he strangled it even harder, forcing its head away from him. The snake tightened its grip more, this time exerting its fiercest pressure yet, which nearly stopped his heart, nearly choked off his breath. A bone somewhere in his spinal area and another one by his right elbow gave a crack one right after the other. His left arm, meanwhile, was growing more and more fatigued. He clenched his jaw. There was a fire in his eyes, and silently he swore at it: *You scum beast! You species of shit! You ugly ogre! Me or you, who's it going to be?* But the cursing did him no good at all. It weakened him, even, because it rang hollow—the truth was, he was contemplating letting go of its neck and surrendering. He made himself walk on. His torso felt shrunken and hunched forward from the weight and pressure of the snake.

As they passed back by the Goddess's shrine near the pond, the giant snake tautened its grip once again —it was as though it could tell its nest was nearby— but he fought back, choking it as hard as he could. For the first time, he thought he could feel his fingers meet around its neck, and he felt as though he was crushing its bones in his very hands. But he was probably deluding himself. He knew full well it was still alive because the force of its constriction remained merciless, and its tail section, now wrapped only around his left leg, still wiggled and moved from side to side. He eyed its head, eyed its upper portion spiraled around his left arm that then ran under his left armpit over to his right shoulder and roped that shoulder and arm and his trunk together with four loops and continued downward, ringing his hips with yet another loop. Even then, it still had a lot of length left. Its lower end, between his two legs, was twined around the left one down to the calf. Because the snake's weight was unevenly distributed, more of it being borne by his left half, he was veering to the left when he walked. He had to fight to keep a straight course along the path. The cut above his right eyebrow continued to bleed, and the scent and taste of blood were still very much present in his nostrils and mouth. He spat again. Though he couldn't see its color in the darkness, he knew his spit remained red.

The giant snake was exceedingly close to him. He'd never imagined his face and a snake's would ever be within such an intimate distance. There had been no portents: not in waking life, not in a dream. Where was its heart? Why couldn't he feel its heartbeat at all? What color might its venom be? White like milk or yellow like amber? How much might it weigh, give or take? Fifty kilograms? Sixty? Seventy? He couldn't tell. But he was sure it outweighed him. In his life, a childhood spent in the fields, he'd come across plenty of snakes before, and snakes of different varieties, but never had he encountered one as big as this king cobra. The question he could hardly dare to ask himself was: was this creature a regular snake, or was it a snake belonging to the Goddess of Praeknamdang? It had, after all, made its appearance right in front of the Goddess's shrine. At that thought, his knees felt like they were going to give, and he . . . he felt utterly lonely. The snake gave a squeeze once again, not as hard this time, then it slackened, though of course not to the point of setting him loose. It was clear the snake wasn't in the slightest considering sparing its enemy's life, it was clear the creature thought with its instincts, and if it could speak, it would probably have the same choice words for him as he'd had for it earlier: *You scum beast! You species of shit! You ugly ogre! Me or you, who's it going to be?*

And as he walked on, eking out slow and difficult steps, he remembered the creepy, peculiar stories he'd heard about king cobras (if truth be told, he wished he didn't have these stories in his head, but he hadn't been able to forget them). His father was the one who'd recounted those stories to him, not to scare him but to teach him to be careful should he ever need to have anything to do with king cobras or other venomous snakes. His father had told him how, when he was a lad of only eighteen, one night in early summer—which was when water in the paddies would be receding and puddles big and small would crop up everywhere, and in those puddles would be trapped hordes and hordes of fish—he had been on his way home from a likay performance at the temple when he heard a strange noise, like somebody was bailing water out of their paddy with a choang loang. But it was already midnight by then; could anybody be so industrious? The sound seemed to come from a puddle in the brush near the old pond, the same pond by which Song Waad would later have the shrine built. His father, once he was sure he had a good grip on his glaive, approached the sound, the whole time keeping his feet light and quiet. What he saw made him choke back a gasp: a huge king cobra, almost four meters in length, had its head end corkscrewed around a tree next to the puddle, its tail end corkscrewed around another tree on the opposite side, and was swinging its body furiously and repeatedly to whip water out of the puddle so it could get to the fish and frogs in there and eat them. The creature was obviously ravenous and in the foulest of moods, so his father thought he had better retreat—and quietly. Given his current predicament, the boy with the bad arm couldn't help but wonder: could the big king cobra his father had encountered that day be the same creature as the one wrapped around his body now?

His father had told him, too, how when he was twenty-one years old and a conscript stationed at the Phra Jomglao military base in town, every Friday afternoon he used to ask his commander for leave so he could go home and visit his mother, who'd been left living alone in Praeknamdang. He would set out on foot from the base and wend his way through various villages and districts, reaching Praeknamdang close to the break of dawn. During those journeys, the only weapon of any kind he would have on him was a glaive, sharp and gleaming. One night, within a patch of scrubland surrounded by fields, his father all of a sudden found himself face to face with a king cobra two meters in length. He and the snake were only an arm's distance apart by the time he noticed it. That king cobra shot up and rocked itself from side to side, spread its hood wide, drew its head back a little bit and—as certain to happen as death—moved to strike immediately. His father swung out his glaive as hard as he could. The snake's blood splattered all over his face, and he then saw its headless body convulsing on the ground. In shock, he stood there staring at the writhing king cobra he'd just decapitated. By the skin of his teeth, he'd come out of the confrontation alive, and out of curiosity, he decided to poke around looking for the snake's severed head, which had gone missing in the poor light of the waning moon. Still clutching the shaft of his glaive, its blade now bloodied, his father walked around in the pale moonlight, his eyes roving up and down. Given his youth at the time, he had a death-or-glory attitude, and he wanted to find that snake's head to keep as a trophy for himself, seeing how the beast had nearly claimed him as its sacrificial victim. He searched and searched for a long time. Eventually he gave up and decided to resume his journey, though he was still sorry not to have found the thing. He'd already walked on for a bit when he noticed that something felt funny—there was an object clinging to the collar of his military uniform, an object that was cold, slippery and raw-smelling. He tore the thing off his shirt: sure enough, it was the king cobra's head, its fangs having been a mere knuckle away from his neck.

His father had also told him how, back when his parents were only two years wed and he was just a baby, three months old, there'd been one evening in the monsoon season, close to nightfall, when his father went out to drain their nursery plot. Then, as he was walking home through a dense thicket of cogon grass, he ran into a king cobra about as thick as his arm. For a king cobra, it wasn't very big, but what it lacked in size it made up for in speed and agility. In the heat of the moment, his father managed to get his hands on a broken branch, and he whacked that snake full force in the middle of its back—the branch snapped in half right in his hands. The king cobra then slithered off and disappeared into the grass. As for his father, he simply went home, built a fire for the oxen to keep the mosquitoes at bay, ate dinner, showered, and went to bed, not giving the cobra a second thought. In the middle of that night, though, he was woken by a strange noise, like something landing on the ground with a thud. For a while it was quiet, but then the noise returned. His father looked over at him—who, remember, was only three months old—and he was sound asleep on his cushion, and then looked over at his mother on the other side of the mattress, and she too was sound asleep. His father grabbed a flashlight and tiptoed down the stairs towards where the noise was coming from. With the flashlight switched on, he saw, by the pillar directly below where the whole family slept, a king cobra the size of his arm, with welts across its back. There was no mistaking it; its scales and injuries betrayed it as the same snake his father had beaten broken-backed earlier that night, and the creature, fueled by revenge, was tenaciously trying to crawl its way up the pillar into the house. But after making it up about three forearms in height, it came crashing down onto the ground with a thud. Still, it tried again, paying no heed to the beam of light shining on its body. That king cobra had struggled over from the spot where it had been beaten and, bearing both pain and a vendetta, had stalked his father all the way home in a quest to settle scores with its fangs. His father said that his body was covered in goosebumps at the sight of that snake. He said, too, that the king cobra might not have been after his life alone, but perhaps the life of his son, and that of his wife as well. His father said he beat that serpent to death without much trouble, but he came away from the experience warier than ever of king cobras and other venomous snakes.

King cobras, his father had said, are at their most ferocious when they're mating. Anyone who happens across a pair of them in the act had better run—and fast. The snakes are sure to be livid, they're sure to stop copulating immediately, and then both of them are sure to come after the person who dared to intrude on their private moment.

His father had also said that one time, when he was twenty-five, he'd used a cruel and unusual method to kill a king cobra. He'd had to kill it because it had bitten someone—a relative of his—while the man was foraging for bamboo shoots in a stream-side grove somewhere among the fields. It happened that the shoot he was trying to dig up was near its nest, and so the snake bit him in the calf and he died on the spot, the spade he'd been using still in his hand. This particular king cobra was a female one. It had only laid four eggs when his father decided to kill it as revenge. His father told his friends to get a big fire going in the common in the middle of the village, and to tend to the fire to make sure it stayed blazing the whole time. As for him, he headed out to that same bamboo grove by the stream, also with a spade in hand. To drive the snake out of its burrow he built a small fire nearby, which alarmed and infuriated it. Although it fled its nest, the snake stayed close to its eggs, not abandoning its territory. Quickly, his father dug into its nest with the spade he'd brought, grabbed the egg that rested at the peak of the pile—its so-called top egg—cast the spade aside, and hotfooted it away. What he'd dared to do was nothing short of snatching a king cobra's top egg in broad daylight. The snake, seeing its egg abducted, rushed to chase after him. Through the open fields, fresh after the harvest, and through the shimmering haze of that day's punishing sun, his father, then in his prime, ran at full tilt, with the king cobra, head reared high, on his heels. The distance between him and the snake kept shrinking. When his father saw that his lead had become so small he might be in trouble—and that he wasn't going to be able to keep up the pace—he removed his hat, tossed it aside and stopped to take a break. He was able to do so because, for the time being, the snake's attention had been diverted to the hat, which the snake now struck at again and again. It took the snake a good while to realize the hat was not its true target, at which point it began pursuing his father once more. That day, his father said, he'd had to shed three of the articles he was wearing so he could give himself three separate breaks: first, the hat; second, the khao ma sash tied around his waist; and third, the shirt on his back, a black farmer's shirt. In each instance, after viciously attacking the object, the king cobra would again be back on his heels. His father was out of breath, and nearly out of steam too, by the time he reached the big, blazing fire on the village common. He then threw the king cobra's prized egg—which was stark white and a little smaller than a chicken egg—into the flames, and with sweat-stung eyes he watched the snake, completely unshrinking, rush headlong into the fire after its egg, and there he watched it thrash and squirm as it was burned to ashes on the blazing logs.

RECALLING THOSE STORIES, the boy grew even more scared, which further diminished his strength. His legs and his left arm felt fatigued; his left hand and all five of its fingers the same. His trunk was even more shrunken now, even more bowed, from the weight of the snake. What would happen if he let go of the giant snake's neck and allowed fate to take charge? In that moment, what he felt was bitter resentment. He wouldn't be intimidated by this snake, no, if only he had a functioning right arm. He'd gladly wrestle it, and he'd crush it to a pulp. Not that he'd expect an easy victory, but he thought in the end he'd be able to defeat it. He tried moving his right arm and tried wiggling the fingers on his right hand—in his desperation, he was hoping for a miracle. Nothing. That whole arm and the hand, strapped to his torso by the snake, remained as stiff and useless as ever.

The village wasn't far now. He staggered on along the ox-cart path—the route was one he knew like the back of his hand. What time was it now? Seven? Seven thirty? Surely before eight. Were it any other day, by this hour he'd already have put his oxen away in their shed, already brought them water, already fetched them straw, and he, probably he would have eaten by now and showered by now, and maybe he'd be kicking back listening to the radio, waiting for it to turn eight thirty, when the Kaew Fah radio theater troupe would come on—they were doing Phanom Tian's *Chulatreekoon*, and they'd left off as the plot was getting exciting—and maybe he'd while away the rest of the evening at one or another of his friends' places, playing a couple of games of checkers. But tonight, everything was different.

His house sat at the edge of the village, giving right onto the fields. He walked into his yard, stopping under the Manila tamarind tree. His house was an old, Thai-style home—a simple, single structure. Up inside, it was quiet and dark. The house looked deserted. *What now?* he wondered. Why had he come home? Why had he come back to the village? He supposed he just didn't know where else to go. He did want to check on his eight oxen, and there must be *someone* in the village able to help him, not that he'd given any thought to how. He walked over towards the cattle shed, not intending to get too close, not meaning to show himself. Instead, he kept out of sight next to the haystack and sneaked a sidelong look at his animals—he was able to count all eight. One or another of his friends must have steered them back to the shed, and that person appeared to have already given them drink and fodder. In the shed, each ox was in its usual spot, each tethered as it should be, and the gate was properly closed. That was a relief to him.

He followed the footpath further. The entire village was dark and quiet. Some of the dogs he walked past started to bark, but they soon quieted down. There were still strong winds coming from the fields. In the sky, tens or maybe even hundreds of thousands of stars shone and twinkled. Blood was still trickling out of the wound above his right eyebrow, its trail running over his eye, over the apple of his cheek and down under his jaw, but he now barely noticed the gamey smell of blood in his nose and mouth. He saw torchlight and could faintly hear the chatter of conversation coming from the pavilion in the center of the village, so he headed that way. He figured that his friends must have spread the word about what had happened to him, and indeed they had.

Just about everyone from the village was gathered there, and they were conferring. Some of them were saying they were going to go and find his parents at the temple to inform them of the terrible news. Some of them were saying they were going to search for him in the fields and then do what was in their power to try to help him. There, in the big, level dirt lot that was their village common, under a mango tree an arm span in girth that stood near the large, generations-old, sala-style pavilion, were gathered both men and women, elderly people as well as children. Some of these people stood, while some sat, gathered into a loose crowd. The light from their torches revealed their eyes and their faces, some of which expressed terror, some concern, some defiance, some disbelief, and others plain curiosity. The men held weapons in their hands: some were armed with knives, some with glaives, some with batons, and others with handguns or rifles.

When he stepped out of the darkness with the giant snake, the crowd instinctively drew closer together, their jabber brought to an abrupt halt. As he approached them, they backed away, either squealing or stuttering, at once awestruck and terrified. Then someone scurried out from among them, dropped down to the ground and prostrated himself.

It was none other than Song Waad.

Seeing Song Waad do as he did, several of the others followed his lead. Among those to sink down and prostrate themselves was Grannie Pluppleung. And then Song Waad, in a voice loud and raspy, announced to the crowd: 'There it is, the snake of the Goddess of Praeknamdang! You see? The Goddess has sent her snake to punish those who scorn her!' Right away, the boy could see how the crowd was swayed by Song Waad and fell in line with his verdict. Among those to be swayed by his words and fall in line with the rest was Grannie Pluppleung. With his face covered in sweat and blood, his eyes hardened into a wide stare, his hair standing up from his head like thorns and his body ringed around and around by the king cobra, he appeared completely altered. Motionless, he stood in front of the crowd, his body banked forward, towards the left. Above him, the stars continued to shine, and the wind from the southeast continued to blow hard. By his left leg, near the calf, the tip of the giant snake's tail continued to sway from side to side. A barn owl flew by, dragging out a long screech before it vanished into the dark. He was silent. He wanted to explain that he'd come back to ask for help, but he couldn't get the words out. He wanted too to thank whoever had helped guide his oxen back to their shed, but he couldn't get those words out either. For some time, the crowd, too, remained silent.

Eventually, a middle-aged man holding a rifle stepped skittishly forward. His gun was cocked, his finger in position on the trigger. The man studied him and the snake up close—from the front, the left, the back and the right—eyeing them timorously all the while. The other men soon followed suit, but it was plain to see that the sheer enormity of the snake made them

all shudder. And they then began talking among themselves once more (naturally, there were words of pity
in the mix as well): *Would it be possible for a group of us
to grab the snake's neck and pry its tail off the boy, at least
to relieve some of the pressure? Would it be possible in one
go for us to grab its neck and slice its throat with a sharp
knife? But would being slashed like that cause the snake
to contract, perhaps even to the point of asphyxiating the
child? Or would it be possible in one go for us to grab its
neck and blow its head off, let's say, with a single bullet?
But would getting shot like that cause the snake to contract, perhaps also to the point of asphyxiating the child?
We ought to settle fast on the means we're going to go with,
and whichever it is, who's going to volunteer? Who's going
to make the first move? And most importantly, don't forget
it's a poisonous snake! And possibly a snake sent by the
Goddess of Praeknamdang!*

At that point, Song Waad walked up to join the
group. He appeared to be in full possession of himself
again. His demeanor was firm and full of fortitude, and
his voice was calm. Ever since he had become a medium,
whatever he did, his actions had always been more

correct than other people's; whatever he said, his words had always been more correct than other people's. He was keenly aware of his status as the village's spiritual leader, a status that placed him on equal standing with— or even higher than—Luang Paw Tien, who was well into his dotage and ailing. Everybody knew the medium was powerful, and he, better than anyone, understood the extent of his power. When he spoke, everybody had to listen, and right then, he began to speak. He talked slowly, making sure his every word was clear:

"This snake belongs to the Patron Goddess of Praeknamdang—the wise needn't but glance out of the corner of their eye to recognize the fact. Whoever dares to lay a hand on the snake will be met with doom. This child has long shown contempt towards the Goddess, both behind closed doors and out in the open, to the point that the Goddess can no longer forgive him. The punishment he's received, really, is more lenient than what he deserves. Let the Goddess's wishes be. So is my advice. And for the sake of the sacred spirit of the Goddess of Praeknamdang, may there be none among you who holds an opinion otherwise."

Song Waad stepped closer to him, closer than anybody else had dared. The medium stared straight into his eyes, and he stared back, unrattled. In those eyes of Song Waad's, the boy could see a smirk of victory. He alone knew it was the victory of a spectacular con artist. He knew now that his prayer to Mae Phra Kongka this past Loy Krathong night—*May I be rid of my hatred of Song Waad, and may he be rid of his hatred of me*—had been in vain. And then every part of his being fell limp and spent.

He turned away from the crowd and began to stagger away. People followed him, thronging around him from a safe distance. His stooped body and the dark, lustrous scales of the snake were awash in the light of their torches. He felt so depleted that he could bear it no more. He realized now there was nobody left he could count on. And in that second, he shrieked at the top of his lungs, relinquished the snake's neck from his left grip, let out a sigh and dropped his head in surrender.

The giant king cobra's neck folded as soon as he released his hand. Its entire length was limp and lifeless. The creature was dead. Since when, nobody could say.

People gathered around the boy and helped to peel and pull off its coils, which fell away with ease. They were still in awe of—and still made nervous by—the snake's gargantuan size, and by turns they began making this and that observation. But nothing and no one mattered anymore to the boy with the bad arm. His eyes were vacant. At times he smiled, at times he laughed, at times he cried, at times he mumbled to himself. He'd lost his mind the moment he'd decided to surrender.

AFTERWORD

by Mui Poopoksakul

Saneh Sangsuk was ten years old—in other words, the same age as the unlucky boy cruelly nicknamed Gimp—in 1967, the approximate year in which *Venom* is set. Read by itself, *Venom* does not tell us when the story takes place, but it does tell us where: the village of Praeknamdang. The setting, a fictionalized version of the author's own birthplace in the Thai province of Phetchaburi, serves as a frequent backdrop in Sangsuk's body of work, linking the story to the larger universe and cast of characters he has created. By cross-referencing *Venom* with his other tales set in Praeknamdang, we know our boy with the bad arm would have been a contemporary of the author, would have played with the other village children that people his other works, and one of those children would, indeed, grow up to become a writer: the narrator of Sangsuk's debut novel, *White Shadow*.

White Shadow is often described as an auto-biographical novel (although it is so only in very broad strokes and in very granular details). Like his alter ego in it, Sangsuk came of age during the heyday of Thai social realism, known locally as the "art for the sake of life" movement (in contrast to art for the sake of art), and its mandate was for literature to serve (Marxist) ideology. Sangsuk himself was not immune to the movement's pull, and published at least one early story in that vein, but he ultimately rejected it, pointedly choosing to write his first novel as a stream-of-consciousness narrative—pointedly, that is, choosing to look inward rather than outward. (Not coincidentally, the narrator of *White Shadow* is a selfish young man who abandons his home village of Praeknamdang, refusing to take up the cause of the farmers he grew up among.) Sangsuk has explained that he does not believe literature can bring about social change, at least not in a country like Thailand, where, he said, the reading culture is too weak and writers are not held up as thinkers. But it was not his recalcitrance toward the political left that earned him the moniker "literary renegade" early in his career. It was conservatives that dubbed him so because his first novel, deemed too offensive to moral standards for the SEA Write Award, ran counter to Thailand's propaganda-imposed self-image as a good and beautiful society where people happily wave the flag for Nation, Religion, and Monarchy.

For Sangsuk, writing is, instead, a personal act. He has stated that when writing he always has an intended reader in mind, an intended addressee. Even more than that, his prose tends to have the immediacy of speech, and, as intricate as it can be, tends to have a spoken rhythm and logic to it. His narrators, indeed, often "speak" to a specific "listener" or group of "listeners." In *White Shadow*, for example, there are two "you"s as the protagonist alternately addresses himself and a past lover. In *The Understory*, the novel Sangsuk deems his masterpiece, Luang Paw Tien (whom we meet here in *Venom*) tells his fireside tales to the children of Praeknamdang (not that Sangsuk minds if anybody else wants to listen in). Here in *Venom*, the narrator retells himself his father's stories about snakes and, of course, performs for his friends, reciting a poem from a nineteenth-century epic parody called *Eng Ting Hao*, by a poet whose pen name was Talok Woharn (which loosely translates to "Funny Wordsmith").

The immediacy of Sangsuk's voice has, over his career, morphed in form from stream of consciousness to a new favorite device: oral storytelling. The self-absorbedness of youth has given way to something more communal, more connected to his heritage. Sangsuk wrote *White Shadow* when he was still living in Bangkok, where he studied and worked for nearly twenty years, from the late 70s to the mid-90s. During that period, he, like the city, was "West-facing," as he himself characterizes it. He wrote his Praeknamdang-set works, including *Venom* and *The Understory*, only after he had moved home to Phetchaburi and turned his gaze back toward his own birthplace. He had missed home, he said about writing those books.

Venom—probably his best-known work alongside *White Shadow*—is a story that combines a few of his traits: his belief in the power and purpose of stories to entertain, his contempt for blind reverence, and his love for the village of his youth. By the time the author returned home for good, however, the place of his birth and boyhood had changed, transformed by the forces of time and capitalism—Thai readers of Sangsuk's work have often remarked how Praeknamdang is a depiction of a Thai village from a bygone era. If Sangsuk is always writing to or for someone, it seems, at least to this translator, that his Praeknamdang books are a series of missives—love letters, though his love can be tough— penned to and for his hometown, a place once real that no longer exists, a place preserved in time through his fiction, a place that was once the center of the universe for a child named Saneh, who might have played with a boy with a bad arm.

EXTRACT FROM
THE UNDERSTORY

by Saneh Sangsuk, translated by Mui Poopoksakul

The night was cold and quiet and drab, like every night that early winter in Praeknamdang. The season's chilly winds had arrived, but were yet to launch a full assault; for now, they were only a persistent trickle, a constant waft, chapping-dry and soundless, an insinuation of the coming brutality, a nascent harshness lurking in the cool air that slithered through the trees. The later the hour, the more sluggish the breeze grew, but somehow the bitter and dry quality about the air only magnified, and it seeped into every particle that made up the land and the sky, the streams and the swamps, and made up those sweeping, forlorn paddy fields, green brushed with yellow, which seemed to glow all on their own under the light from the stars and moon, and it seeped into everything there was, from shrubbery and the chains of toddy palms forming an undulating line on the horizon, to houses and huts, to the breaths drawn by all the domesticated animals and their human masters. It was a year the floods rose high enough to sweep into the yard of every home in Praeknamdang—no matter that the village was located on a tract of upland—and the turbid, white water took a long time subsiding. People herded their cattle and pigs to places of even higher elevation; they moored their boats right at their front steps and seized the chance to fish right in their own yards, and everybody caught copious amounts of different kinds of fish, which they smoked or cured with salt or fermented and kept in jars large and small. But the paddy crops had suffered no small degree of damage. The surviving rice plants came up tall and stringy like climbers, and when they sprouted ears, they were populated by small, deflated grains rather than the usual, plump ones, and all that season, there wasn't a child in Praeknamdang who got to eat any pandan rice pudding at all, however much they begged their mothers or grandmothers to make them some. It was the animals who first sensed the deluge and the calamity it would bring. Bees built their hives only on high-up branches; baya weavers too built their nests on high-up branches; serpents and other such creatures, both poisonous and not, flocked to hillocks or rises or tall trees; and green tree ants grew wings and began to fly about, relocating their nests to areas they thought beyond the flood's reach. The people of Praeknamdang paid heed to the animals and relayed what they were seeing to one another, to their children and grandchildren, and could foresee the situation they were about to face, the hardships they would have to bear and the struggles that were in store for them. It was a night near the end of December in 2510 BE, or 1967 CE, and the tam kwan khao ceremonies for the Goddess of Rice had come and gone, this time mirthless occasions without the usual fanfare, even subdued like a funeral, but the harvest season hadn't yet arrived. For the people of Praeknamdang, it was a period of rest. Everyone among them was somber, in despair and miserable, weighed down by all the problems such as there were. All the physical and mental effort that they had dedicated to their land during the planting season would, it was now clear, prove practically pointless. Even the children were somber, in despair and miserable as

78

they observed their parents sighing and venting to one another in hushed tones. It was a year when Chartchai Chionoi was still the world flyweight champion, a year when Suraphol Sombatcharoen was still alive and still crooning and writing songs, putting out hit after smash hit, a year when Mitr Chaibancha was still alive and still playing the leading man in seemingly hundreds of motion pictures. It was the year the people of Praeknamdang were abuzz about Shah Pahlavi of Iran's upcoming visit to Thailand and the preparations for Emperor Haile Selassie of Ethiopia's visit to Thailand and the earlier official visit to Thailand of Lyndon B. Johnson, President of the United States of America (all news learned from the radio). It was a year when the young ladies emulated Petchara Chaowarat's fashion, dressing themselves in blouses and pants, and emulated her hairstyle as well, and a year young men across Thailand went wild for the Twist and the Watusi; the young men in Praeknamdang, too, knew their way around these dances, because a traveling ram wong troupe had introduced them to the people there. It was the year the radio theater group Kaew Fah was at the height of its fame and its *Blessing of Brahma* and *Farmhouse Angel* and *Gem in the Slums* were on-air, to all of which the people of Praeknamdang were incorrigibly addicted. It was a year when the novel *House of Golden Sand* was still a bestseller, and its sequel *Pojaman Sawangwong* was still a bestseller, and *Lonely Road* was still a bestseller, which catapulted K. Surangkanang to the position of Thailand's number one smith of words, and she would remain popular for a long time to come, even though the writer-critic self-styled as "The Grouch" had already issued the following sarcastic advice to the author: "If I were K. Surangkanang, I would have combined these three novels into one and renamed the whole tome *Pojaman Sawangwong on a Lonely Road Behind the House of Golden Sand.*" It was the year the only son of Kraam Kichagood, the latter the owner of a large herd of cattle and Praeknamdang's village chief, was preparing to go and continue his education in town, which meant he had better opportunities in life than the other children in Praeknamdang of his age group, nearly all of whom received only a third-grade education. It was a year when the great lady Ms. Prayong Sisan-ampai still taught at the local Praeknamdang Temple School, still harbored big hopes and big dreams for the children of Praeknamdang, her pupils, when she imagined their futures: that when they grew up, they would possess fulgent and beautiful spirits, like the one Ms. Prayong herself had, and entertain big hopes and big dreams, like she herself did, and never in their lives allow themselves to become creatures of despair, no matter how much and how often misery would be theirs to endure. It was the year the Venerable Father Tien Thammapanyo, or Luang Paw Tien, the abbot of Praeknamdang Temple, turned ninety-three years old, and was seventy-three years into his monkhood . . .

Saneh Sangsuk (b. 1957) is an award-winning Thai author, known locally by his pen name Dan-arun Saengthong. He is regarded in Thailand as one of the greatest writers of his generation, having written multiple acclaimed novels and story collections. He is a highly prolific literary translator, working under different pen names, and counts Ernest Hemingway, Edgar Allan Poe, Oscar Wilde, Franz Kafka, Gabriel García Márquez, and Knut Hamsun among the numerous authors he has translated. In 2014, he won Thailand's coveted SEA Write Award for *Venom and Other Stories* (อสรพิษและเรื่องอื่นๆ), a collection that includes some of his best-known stories. In 2018, the Thai government awarded him the title of National Artist for his contributions to the country's literature, and he has also been named a Chevalier de l'Ordre des Arts et des Lettres by the French government. Sangsuk lives in Phetchaburi, in a small village similar to the fictional Praeknamdang, where many of his tales are set. *Venom* and *The Understory* are the first of his works to be published in the United States.

Mui Poopoksakul is a lawyer-turned-translator. She was awarded a PEN/Heim Translation Fund grant for her translation of Sangsuk's *The Understory* and also received a PEN Translates grant from English PEN for her translation of *Venom*. Mui's other translations include works by contemporary Thai authors Prabda Yoon and Duanwad Pimwana, and she has contributed widely to literary journals since she began her translation career. A native of Bangkok who spent two decades in the U.S., she now lives in Berlin, Germany.